Avatar

Avatar

Evan Lavender-Smith

SIX GALLERY PRESS
PITTSBURGH, PA

An excerpt from this book appeared in *elimae*

ISBN-10 1-926616-16-2
ISBN-13 978-1-926616-16-2

LIBRARY OF CONGRESS CIP DATA
AVAILABLE UPON REQUEST

Six Gallery Press
P.O. Box 90145
Pittsburgh, PA 15224

To Richard Greenfield

You always need one more light positively to identify another. Imagine it quite dark and then one point of light appears; you would be quite unable to place it, since no spatial relation can be made out in the dark. Only when one more light appears can you fix the place of the first, in relation to it.

Søren Kierkegaard

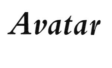

Avatar

they were my friends for a great number of years they were my greatest friends they floated alongside me to keep me company they were the first great friends I made here I would awaken from sleep I would awaken after a night of sleep or after a day of sleep I would awaken to find my tears still floating at my side I would be overjoyed upon awakening having opened my eyes to find thousands of tears thousands of old friends still faithfully floating alongside no matter how lonely no matter how tormented I might later suggest to have felt during this period no matter were I later to suggest having experienced only terrible loneliness throughout the duration of this period I would not have been correct in so saying I would not have been correct because I had my tears in so saying I would have failed to remember my tears for they remained with me all the while all the while during this period which if I remember correctly overlapped with another period a period during which I concentrated my efforts exclusively upon the nature of space the nature of empty space to be precise my thinking of which was of course reflected in the subject of our conversations our conversations being one way conversations conversations proceeding from me in the direction of my tears never from my tears in the direction of me tears being unable to speak this first period by which I mean that very lengthy period a great number of years before my ducts went dry a period which included so many one way conversations one way conversations between me and my tears this first period having coincided with a second period a period during which I focused my thoughts exclusively on the nature of empty space or so it is called it is called empty space however I still feel confident I still feel relatively confident when I say when I think to say that the empty space may in fact not be entirely empty it was during this coincidence of periods a period of my tears floating faithfully by my side and a period of concentrating my efforts exclusively upon the nature of the so called empty space when I would time and again attempt and fail to recall what it was I had forgotten with respect to the fact of the so called empty space between the stars not actually being empty the black space the apparent uniform blackness between the stars in fact not actually being empty the coincidence or the overlapping of two periods before my ducts went dry a very great number of years that great number of years during which I would repeatedly attempt and fail to recall what it was I had forgotten with respect to the existence of so many stars of so very many stars such that every point at which I look in the so called empty space between the stars there should in fact be another star at that very point very far away so that if it were not for this something or other this something or other notwithstanding this something or other the nature of which I had forgotten the nature of which I continue to forget this something or other between me and all the distant stars if not for the singular phenomenon of this particular something or other then the empty space would at all times appear entirely white entirely bright with stars entirely bright with starlight there being so many stars so very many stars that every point at which I look in the blackness somewhere along my line of sight somewhere within the great depths of darkness there should be a star at that precise point very far away the so called empty or black space between the stars appearing empty or black on account of this something or other being there to prevent the starlight from reaching me the forgotten nature of this something or other being perhaps similar to the nature of a shield a shield of some sort standing between us a shield to block the light from all those millions all those billions of distant stars these something or others standing between us these shields of which I used to know something but have since forgotten everything or nearly everything of course not everything not entirely everything for I do remember one thing I still remember at least one thing I still remember the existence of the something or others I still remember that these something or others do in fact simply exist it is only their nature I have forgotten their specific character the specific character of their shielding nature therefore it may be that I will again remember their specific character so long as I continue to remember that they do simply exist I must not under any circumstance allow myself to forget that they do in fact exist I must never forget that there are many more stars than just these two one night or one day while I am sleeping while I am concentrating my efforts upon the star in front of me the nature of the existence of the something or others might suddenly be revealed might suddenly be reawakened within me and in that case I will then feel first hand confidence or first hand relative confidence in saying or in thinking of saying that because of the specific nature because of the specific character of the shields recently reawakened within me which specific character I will then proceed to describe in detail because of this specific character the light from all those billions of distant stars is not making it to my eyes therefore I mistakenly perceive the empty space to be black instead of white I mistakenly perceive a blackness which has absolutely nothing at all to do with emptiness but simply with the fact that I am looking at the backs of all the shields the backs of all the something or others and were I able to somehow glimpse the fronts of the shields the fronts of the something or others I would find that the front of each shield gleams like a star and I would in that case feel first hand confidence first hand relative confidence instead of the second hand relative confidence I now feel because I have forgotten I have simply forgotten a detail like having forgotten the name of something without having forgotten the existence of the something itself so I still feel even now some degree some slight degree of second hand relative confidence when saying when thinking of saying that there was a time in the past when I felt first hand relative confidence in my certain or in my relatively certain knowledge of the nature of the existence of the something or others likewise I still feel some slight degree of second hand relative confidence in saying or in thinking of saying that where I am now is at a distant location a very distant location perhaps an extremely distant location from where I was before before I arrived here I am able to say this to think this with relative confidence because where I am now I see two stars looking around in every direction I see only two yet I know there are more or I must at least assume there are because of the confidence the first hand relative confidence I remember having once felt when saying or thinking or when thinking of saying that there is something or other between my eyes and all the distant stars I can therefore still feel some degree of confidence although only a very slight degree of second hand relative confidence in remembering that I once felt great confidence great first hand relative confidence in saying or in thinking in thinking of saying that the so called empty space is not so empty after all therefore it is entirely possible perhaps even entirely likely that I am in the same general place the same general world as I was before before I came here before I arrived here because where I was before on the roof I could see thousands of stars where I am now only two where I was before I could see thousands of stars from atop the roof from atop my roof or perhaps not from atop my roof perhaps not from atop mine but rather from atop my parents from atop my parents roof if I remember correctly I could see thousands of stars from atop my parents roof yet I am no longer confident or even relatively confident that I know what I mean by the word roof when I say or think to say from atop the roof for it has been a long while a very long while since I have been in contact with a roof the thing the word roof points at likewise a very long while since I have been inside a what is it called or walked up a staircase quite a long while since I have walked up a staircase what I would now give for a staircase a flight of stairs to come upon a flight of stairs a little staircase it would not necessarily have to lead anywhere only a few steps carpeted steps a carpeted staircase floating by I would lay my head on a step fall asleep and dream about stairs about carpeted stairs a carpeted staircase only a few steps what I would give but what I mean to say I know or what I mean to say I know with relative confidence is that where I was before I could see many stars where I am now only two therefore I must be very far very distant from where I was before but not necessarily out of reach of where I was before I can say or I can think to say with relative confidence that beyond the so called empty space may be those same stars those many thousands of stars from before from the roof but I cannot see them because of the presence of the something or others the nature of which I have entirely forgotten or nearly entirely forgotten which nature I can only suspect is related to something about light something about starlight not being light exactly if I remember correctly turning back now to measure something about light about starlight being something more like sand quarter of a fingernail or perhaps about light about starlight being composed not of light not of starlight or not exactly of light turning back but of something else which may be similar to that something of which sand is composed still a quarter of a fingernail as well or anything else for that matter or for that matter that something or other of which anything else is composed or anything else composed of matter for that matter something about light about the composition of starlight being similar to the manner in which a beach may be said to be composed of sand a beach of sand a beach of light a beach of starlight a beach of sand what I would give for sand to stumble upon a couple grains floating by what I would give for some grains of sand to come upon some sand from a beach sand from an ocean I had for a great number of years forgotten the ocean and upon remembering it upon remembering the ocean it became a difficult a very difficult very painful subject there are others like time others like time like the ocean like baseball cards time the ocean baseball cards and of course pinecones the word pinecone to be precise but the ocean is one of the most very difficult one of the most very painful despite the fact that I was never a sailor never a fisherman despite my never having lived near an ocean if I remember correctly in fact I may have only seen the ocean once only one time but at least one time I am sure of it I am sure because I can think of it I can think not only of the word but of what the word means what the word points at the ocean and what a great effect the ocean had on me what a tremendous effect the one time I saw it of course I do not know which ocean I do not remember which specific ocean it was I was very young at the time this was long before I came here long before I arrived here I can no longer name the oceans such a long while since I have been in contact with an ocean atlantis something the atlantis or the titanic the titanic and the atlantis and the antarctic oceans furthermore at one time I knew the capitals of all the states the united states of atlantis now I can name only one tucson I do not know I do not remember however which state it belongs to I used to imagine I used to pretend that instead of floating in the empty space in the so called empty space between my stars I remember pretending to be floating in the ocean imagining or pretending or pretending to imagine coming across something floating by something anything a bottle a bottle floating in the empty space floating in the ocean a bottle with a piece of paper rolled up inside I would open the bottle reach inside to retrieve the rolled up piece of paper and I still after all these years I still remember exactly what the words said the exact words written on the piece of paper when I unrolled it do not lose hope were the words keep on going or something to that effect the words were do not lose hope or do not worry things are going to be okay I remember pretending or imagining or imagining pretending coming across something anything to come across anything a bottle with a rolled up piece of paper inside anything at all just something that would let me know something to give me a second wind go for the gold something to lift my spirits if only for a moment keep your chin up just keep on floating keep on floating toward your star the one in front quarter of a fingernail I wished for something like this quite often at first shortly after I arrived that period those many years an extremely great number of years during which I constantly asked myself questions concerning the nature of my arrival concerning the reason concerning the true reason for my arrival or the true nature the true character of my arrival which period immediately followed that very long period during which I contemplated the nature of the so called empty space that great number of years during which I conversed with my tears a period after my ducts went dry during which I constantly asked myself questions concerning the nature of my arrival questions such as how did I arrive here questions such as why did I arrive here such as why did I arrive here in this place with only two stars a period consumed by questions which seemed to me at the time the most important the most vital questions how did I arrive here why did I arrive here how did I suddenly go from where I was before go from the place in which I had been the place in which I had sat upon my parents roof counting thousands upon thousands of stars questions such as how did I suddenly go from there to here such as to here where I can see only two stars one in front one behind both a quarter of a fingernail exactly why did this happen how could this have happened questions such as what could I have possibly done to get myself in this terrible situation such as what could I have done to allow for this to happen such as to deserve for this to happen I would ask such questions all day long or all night long I would ask them over and over I asked them all throughout this period following the period during which I conversed with my tears I asked my questions a thousand perhaps ten thousand perhaps a million or even ten or even a hundred million or a hundred billion times I asked these questions questions such as how did I arrive here why did I arrive here I asked my questions over and over again so very many times I asked them so very many times until my questions no longer seemed to me like questions but seemed instead like statements after asking myself these questions for so long day after day night after night year after year after asking them so very many times without providing a single answer in reply to a single of my questions it was then perhaps that my questions no longer seemed to me like questions but rather like statements or more specifically seemed like statements of questions more specifically like the simple stating of a question the answer to which is not possible is not available or rather like the simple stating of a question the answer to which is itself the simple stating of the question or rather is itself the next simple stating of the question which is not to say the answer is a simple restating of the question or not to say the answer is already provided in the question in the manner of those questions which are statements only insofar as the question being stated is not intended to be answered but stated only to suggest how obvious the answer is no that is not at all how my questions seemed to me like statements of questions but rather the questions which had become statements of questions seemed to have somehow lost their ability to be questions the questions had become content to accept that no reply would be given and thus become content to shed their questioning nature to instead accept themselves as statements simply as statements without any hope without any need of a reply other than the next statement of the same question which is not to say that my statements of my questions were hopeless or needless in the negative sense but only that my questions were no longer simply my questions but instead simply my statements of my questions statements that did not expect that did not need or did not hope for a reply therefore no need or hope could be upset when no reply came other than of course my next statement of my next question so my questions rather my statements of my questions remained hopeless only in the positive sense which is to say my questions had become positively hopeless my positively hopeless questions had become positively hopeless statements and I was saddened I was greatly saddened by my questions having become positively hopeless statements for I had grown so used to my questions being simply positively hopeless questions having been so for such a great number of years and I grieved the absence of their positively hopeless questioning nature once they became positively hopeless statements of positively hopeless questions for they were all I had at the time this period having followed that period that great number of years during which my tears floated by my side having followed the abrupt disappearance of my tears the great act of abandonment committed against me by my tears my great old friends gone and my questions my positively hopeless questions had during this period become my only friends my very best friends following the disappearance of my tears following their abandonment of me following my ducts going dry and my inability to cry myself more friends to cry myself more tears I had known my positively hopeless questions as questions for so long and to suddenly accept them as positively hopeless statements was extremely difficult very painful at first as I mourned as I grieved the loss of their questioning nature as I mourned the loss of my old friends I say of my questions I think to say of my questions they were good friends they were good companions likewise I think to say of my sneakers of my air jordans they are my friends my companions likewise of my stars and my tears likewise of my fingernails and my arms likewise of my legs and so on I say they are good friends good companions but in so saying or in so thinking of so saying I do not mean to think to say that my tears or my air jordans or my stars my fingernails or my arms my legs my stars or my strands of hair I do not mean to suggest that they are my friends in the same manner that I had friends before where I was before I arrived here when I was atop the roof of my parents what is it called I do not mean to say I do not mean to think to say that I am the friend of my arm for example but I only mean to think to say that my arm is indeed my friend to think to say that the friendship between me and my arm only proceeds one way only in one direction and if my arm could hear me and if I were to ask my arm to proceed to name its very dearest friends and if my arm could speak more than likely my arm would not proceed to count me among its very dearest friends however if my arm could hear and also speak then perhaps our friendship would not be one way but would in that case in the case of my arm being able to hear and speak in that case our friendship would be reciprocal a reciprocal friendship a friendship proceeding both ways perhaps in that case a true friendship however the fact remains that my arm cannot hear and it cannot speak therefore my arm is not my friend in the true sense of the word friend the word friend and the word friendship suggesting a certain amount of effort on the part of both parties involved I say or I think or I think to say that my arm my legs my sneakers my stars my fingernails my strands of hair my tears and so on I think to say that they cannot be my friends in the same manner that I think to say I had friends on the roof because the friendship in this case in the case of my arms and in the case of my sneakers these friendships proceed in only one direction therefore my arm may be my friend to me yet I am not the friend of my arm my arm from its perspective would more than likely not count me among its friends and although I think to say this I cannot remember having had any friends on my roof not on my roof not on my roof rather on my parents roof nevertheless I am confident or I am relatively confident in my understanding of the meaning of the word friendship relatively confident in my understanding of the efforts or the terms required of a true friendship by which I mean that certain amount of effort required on the part of both parties involved in a friendship therefore my sneakers my arms my legs my stars my fingernails my strands of hair my tears and so on cannot be considered my friends in the true sense of the word the true meaning of the word friendship yet I nevertheless consider them my friends I nevertheless consider them my good friends despite the absence of that amount of effort said to be required of them in order to make our friendship a true friendship a reciprocal friendship I am willing to excuse my legs and my arms this required amount of effort I still call them my friends despite this absence of required effort if only because I want them to be my friends and I have no choice but to embrace my air jordans

my arms my legs my tears my stars my strands of hair
and so on as my friends because if I do not excuse
them this effort if I do not consider them my friends
then what else must I consider them but my enemies
my absolute enemies or at the very least strangers
they would in that case be either absolute enemies or
absolute strangers to me and this I could not tolerate
I simply could not tolerate considering my arms and
my legs absolute enemies or absolute strangers for
how could I live comfortably in such proximity to
absolute enemies such proximity to absolute strangers
I would much prefer to simply excuse my arms and
my legs and my air jordans excuse them that lack of
effort required of true friendship so as not to have to
live in what would be such intolerable proximity to
absolute enemies or to absolute strangers however I

might consider not excusing my tears and my strands of hair if only because they turned against me they turned against me when they disappeared so in that case in the case of my tears and my strands of hair there was not only the absence of required effort but also something less than an absence of effort there was an act of absolute abandonment committed by my tears a terrible act of absolute abandonment committed by my strands of hair absolute abandonment being the one act a friend must not commit under any circumstance the one act a friend must not commit if that friend is in the least way concerned with maintaining a friendship one cannot commit an act of absolute abandonment an act of mysterious abandonment against a friend and expect things to one day simply return to normal therefore it cannot be said it cannot truthfully be said of either my tears or my strands of hair it cannot be said that they are or ever were my friends that they were ever truly my friends instead I must consider my tears and my strands of hair my absolute enemies my very worst enemies or at the very least absolute strangers and what I once perceived as a true friendship suffered an act of absolute abandonment on their part which revealed that friendship to be a false friendship false from the very beginning never a true friendship at all however I must say I must think to say I must remember or I must admit that although there is no chance no chance at all of resuming a friendship or even of resuming an acquaintance between us I still must say must think to say I still must admit that I miss them I must admit that I miss them terribly I miss them so very much I miss my tears and my strands of hair despite their behavior despite these despicable acts of absolute abandonment and I pray perhaps not pray but wish I wish there was something I could do something I could say something I could think to say to make them come back to me to encourage my tears and my strands of hair to come back to make them want to come back to me something I could think to say some gesture on my part that would convince them to come back to continue floating by my side to continue floating in front of my face in the case of my strands of hair and continue floating alongside me in the case of my tears to come back not simply for a while not simply for a year or a number of years or a great number of years or even an extremely great number of years but for them to come back for all time for them to truly want to come back for all time not come back because they feel an obligation not because they feel sorry for me in my grief in my terrible grief over these despicable acts of absolute abandonment on their part but because they want to because they truly and deeply desire to return to my side for all time because they would very much enjoy doing so because they would tremendously enjoy doing so however I do not know what that thing would be that thing to say to think to say the one gesture I could make all I can think to say is please to say please come back to think to say to them to my tears my strands of hair to say that the gesture on their part to come back to me to return to floating alongside me for all time this would be an act of such graciousness and I would be so pleased so grateful if you were to come back to me my tears my strands of hair so grateful please please come back today come back tonight yet in saying or in thinking in thinking of saying how grateful I would be upon their return in saying how very much I desire for them to return to my side for all time perhaps in so saying in so thinking of so saying I am so thinking and so saying selfishly for selfish reasons alone their coming back being an act of such graciousness on their part an act to make me overjoyed to feel overwhelmed with joy in so thinking of so saying not taking into consideration how they might feel but only thinking of myself for perhaps they have moved on to other things moved on to better things moved on to make new friends very good friends perhaps so why should I expect why should I ask them to abandon their new friends ask them to commit despicable acts of terrible abandonment against their new friends on account of me for my sake for the sake of someone who only wants to befriend them to rebefriend them selfishly for purely selfish reasons alone for reason of my feeling so alone feeling so terribly lonely on account of the despicable acts of terrible abandonment committed against me of course they should not come back of course they will not come back all this while I thought that our friendships were proceeding only one way only in one direction in the direction of my friends those I called my friends my tears and my strands of hair from me toward them yet perhaps it was exactly the opposite all this while it was that the party involved who acted truly selflessly the party who acted in the manner required of true friendship that party was not me but was in fact my tears was in fact my strands of hair for they asked nothing of me in all those years that great number of years of floating by my side yet I asked so much of them for such a great number of years never stopping never once stopping to question whether I was giving anything back never once stopping to thank my tears and strands of hair for being such good friends for such a great number of years I never once made the necessary effort myself so of course those friendships were doomed they were doomed from the very start doomed because there was only one party exerting the required effort only one party to our friendship who acted selflessly only one party exerting the required effort and that party was certainly not me therefore I do not know what the word friendship means after all it would seem my understanding of the word friendship and the word friend has been mistaken all this while moreover I was the party to our friendship who instigated the first great act of separation between me and my strands of hair not my strands of hair it was my fault not theirs for I must remember my plucking I must remember that period during which I would pluck out strands of hair from my head in order to examine their color to see if their color had changed I have been floating for a very long while for an extremely great number of years yet of course I do not have a mirror to determine the extent to which I have aged I have no way to examine the wrinkles on my face other than with my fingers I have only my fingers the tips of my fingers with which to examine my wrinkles I depress a fingertip into a wrinkle and run the fingertip along the wrinkle in order to gauge if that particular wrinkle has grown in length or in width or in depth since I last measured it but these measurements are never as accurate as one would hope so instead I would pluck out a strand of hair to examine its color in order to compare it with the color I had known my hair to be before I arrived here before I came here when I was on the roof my hair was a reddish brown a nice auburn if I remember correctly so I would pluck out a single strand of hair to examine the color in comparison to that color to see whether or not I had aged since being on the roof on my parents roof and the color of that plucked strand did in fact appear gray one might even say white I had to my surprise plucked out a white strand of hair and then I plucked out another which was just as white then to my surprise another then another each just as white as the last some perhaps even whiter then I plucked another then to my surprise another then to my surprise another and so on until I had plucked out half the hair on my head the left half and for a number of years thereafter I floated among these thousands of white strands of plucked hair these thousands upon thousands of plucked white strands of hair which floated in front of my face in front of my eyes making the task of watching my star while sleeping very difficult extremely difficult I was annoyed I was very upset by this I could not concentrate on my star while I slept I was very upset very annoyed at first I felt that the struggle to keep an eye on my star while I slept had become an intolerable struggle I was very upset about this until one night or one day as I was sleeping feeling very annoyed struggling intolerably to watch the light from my star between these thousands upon thousands of strands of hair in front of my eyes many of which strands often became caught between my eyelid and my eyeball making sleep impossible making sleep simply intolerable until one day or one night as I was struggling to watch my star through all the thousands upon thousands of plucked strands struggling intolerably to do so all of sudden they disappeared they simply disappeared vanished and what I had for so long for a great number of years considered such a great annoyance the source of so much intolerable struggling these thousands upon thousands of strands of white hair that would get caught not only under my eyelids but also in my mouth in my throat and which I often inhaled through my nose these thousands upon thousands of strands of hair this source of so much intolerable struggling was suddenly gone finally gone suddenly lifted from me at last I was finally relieved of the intolerable struggle to keep an eye on my star while sleeping to keep an eye on my star through so many thousands of strands of hair I felt so relieved and for many years thereafter I felt so very relieved so overjoyed to no longer have to struggle so intolerably while I slept but only to have to struggle so much as was necessary in order to keep my eyelids partially opened to keep an eye on my star while sleeping which was of course a struggle a great struggle in fact nearly an intolerable one but so much less intolerable than the intolerable struggle presented by my strands of hair compared to that intolerable struggle the struggle presented by watching my star while I slept to make sure I continued floating in the right direction this struggle compared to the previous one was a comfortable even a welcome struggle quite tolerable indeed however a number of years after I had been relieved of my intolerable struggle a number of years after my strands had suddenly disappeared I began to long for those strands which had caused me so much intolerable struggling I began to miss those thousands upon thousands of strands of white hair in front of my eyes I missed how they had caused me so much intolerable struggling I missed how they had made me struggle so intolerably while I slept I began to miss them intolerably I missed those strands so very intolerably such that keeping an eye on my star while I slept only struggling as much as necessary to keep an eye on my star soon became an intolerable struggle the likes of which I had never known before an intolerable struggle much more intolerable than my old intolerable struggle by which I mean that intolerable struggle following from the thousands upon thousands of strands of white hair blocking my view of my star while I slept much more intolerable than that because now as I slept without those thousands upon thousands of strands blocking my view of my star I was so acutely so intolerably aware of the lack of that old intolerable struggle presented by having to watch the light from my star from between thousands upon thousands of strands now that my strands of hair had abandoned me I found myself missing my old struggle very much I had become friends with that old intolerable struggle I had become very good friends with that particular struggle with my old intolerable struggle my old intolerable struggle had perhaps become one of my few faithful companions one of my few very close friends without my having ever realized it and now that the struggle was gone this new struggle the new intolerable struggle of missing my old intolerable struggle seemed to me much more intolerable than I had ever known my old intolerable struggle to be I found this new struggle simply intolerable with this new intolerable struggle it was impossible to keep myself focused on the light from my star as I slept because I was so acutely aware of the absence of my old intolerable struggle my old best friend and after many years of struggling intolerably at the hand of my new intolerable struggle I decided to go ahead and pluck out all of the hair remaining on my head all the hair on the right side I scattered those many thousands of white hairs before my eyes and soon enough I found myself back to my old intolerable struggle back in the company of my old best friend I had missed so much for such a long while that same good old intolerable struggle represented by my struggling intolerably to keep an eye on the light from my star while I slept between so many thousands upon thousands of white hairs I was overjoyed simply filled with joy for a number of years thereafter for a great number of years in fact I was overwhelmed with joy to have finally regained possession of my old intolerable struggle while I slept and so intolerably did I struggle during those years so intolerably did I struggle to keep an eye on the light from my star once again so very intolerably did I struggle during this period to keep an eye on my star between so many thousands upon thousands of plucked strands just as I had longed for just as I had longed to once again be so intolerably annoyed by my strands before my eyes as I had been for such a great number of years previously that great number of years before my strands of hair had disappeared back when things were simply intolerable and nothing more I was overwhelmed overjoyed to be back to struggling intolerably however within a few years my old intolerable struggle of which I had lately regained possession had once again become intolerable in that very same way the struggle preceding my regaining possession of my old intolerable struggle had been intolerable and before long within only a number of years of having regained possession of my old intolerable struggle my old intolerable struggle had become much more intolerable than that struggle I had experienced when longing for my old intolerable struggle to return my old intolerable struggle was now once again simply intolerable and nothing more simply intolerable merely intolerable and I began to miss to very much miss that intolerable struggle preceding my having regained possession of my current intolerable struggle I again so very much wanted these thousands upon thousands of strands of hair floating in front of my face getting caught beneath my eyelids and in the back of my throat I wanted them gone these thousands of strands blocking my view of my star I wanted them gone at once I longed for them to abandon me once again to abandon me immediately so that I could once again miss my old intolerable struggle intolerably and for a number of years I struggled so intolerably in my longing for these thousands upon thousands of white hairs to disappear to go away these thousands of strands of white hair before my eyes that made watching the light from my star while I slept so difficult how I longed for them to disappear only so that I could long to perhaps regain them once again only to perhaps regain those thousands upon thousands of strands and the old intolerable struggle which accompanied them what I longed for most of all during this period was for my thousands upon thousands of strands to disappear so that I could long for them to one day or one night reappear I struggled intolerably in my longing to once again struggle intolerably in their absence I longed like this for a great number of years until one day or one night I suddenly remembered something about color about the nature of color the true nature of color was reawakened in me I suddenly remembered having once known with confidence with relative confidence I remembered having known that the color of something is determined by the light hitting it I remembered having once felt confident in having known this and I felt that perhaps I could now feel relative confidence or at least second hand relative confidence in saying or in thinking of saying that colors might appear differently here than where I was before atop my roof atop my parents roof I could now feel second hand relative confidence having remembered once feeling confidence relative confidence in my knowledge that color was determined by light and I could now feel some slight degree of second hand relative confidence in saying or in thinking of saying that colors might appear differently here because the light from these two stars might be changing the color of everything from what it used to be or what it would have otherwise been to something different some different color altogether for example my air jordans which used to be white and red if I remember correctly they used to be white and red atop my parents roof but now they appear maroon and white maroon where they used to be white and white where they used to be red maroon and white out here turning now to look my air jordans appear maroon and white out here

between these two stars quarter of a fingernail and
my skin which used to be light before I arrived here
turning back the place I arrived here from the one
with staircases and oceans my skin out here also
appears maroon quarter of a fingernail as well I
suddenly remembered the true nature of light and I
felt that I could again feel confidence relative
confidence at least some degree of second hand
relative confidence in saying in thinking of saying
that the difference in the color of my hair could
perhaps be attributed to a different kind of light the
difference in kinds of light existing between where I
am now the light from these two stars and where I
came here from the place I was before on the roof on
my parents roof where I could see thousands of stars
the light from atop the roof having colored my air

jordans their so called intended colors which is to say that if the sneaker designers who designed my sneakers had known that jordan so and so would be playing baseball out here between these particular two stars they may in that case have used different sneaker coloring dye in order for the sneakers to respond to the light from these two stars as they would have otherwise responded to the light in the place at which the sneaker designers designed the sneakers which is to say respond in the colors white and red so when I again looked at my skin after the true nature of color had been reawakened within me and I saw that my skin was maroon and when I again looked at my air jordans and I saw that my air jordans were not white where they had previously been white but were maroon instead I felt able to feel at least relatively confident in thinking of saying that perhaps these thousands upon thousands of strands of hair floating before me these thousands upon thousands of plucked strands of hair I want so very badly to again disappear to again abandon me again so that I once again might long to struggle intolerably in their absence I felt able to feel at least some slight degree of second hand confidence in saying in thinking of saying that these thousands upon thousands of seemingly white strands of hair might not appear white on the roof on my parents roof in fact my hair color might still be the exact same color it always was the color auburn a nice shade of reddish brown I felt able to feel at least relatively confident in thinking of saying that my surprise when having plucked out that first strand so many years ago that first white strand that my surprise was based on a different kind of light hitting that strand and only making it appear only making it seem white able to feel at least some degree of second hand relative confidence in thinking of saying that all of my intolerable struggling for such a great number of years all of that plucking and struggling was instigated by that initial surprise which was a mistaken surprise a mistaken surprise based on a mistaken perception a mistaken perception which had suggested that my hair had turned completely white second hand relatively confident in saying or in thinking of saying that all of my intolerable struggling was built on a cracked what is it called my hair possibly even probably appearing as nicely auburn as nicely reddish brown as ever under the light from any number of different stars any number of stars other than these particular two and because of my new degree of second hand relative confidence associated with the possibility of my initial surprise following from my mistaken perception that my hair had turned white having been an entirely mistaken perception an entirely mistaken surprise and in my new suspicion that the what is it called was badly cracked my suspicion that all of this plucking all of this struggling was built on a cracked what is it called my intolerable struggling no longer seemed all that intolerable I found myself not longing the way I had before for the return of my intolerable struggle and it was not long after this revelation that my strands again abandoned me disappeared just as I had so long wished for and yet I found myself not longing for their return but instead I had become content to accept only that certain amount of intolerable struggling necessary to keep my eyelids partially opened while I slept in order to keep an eye on the light from my star the one in front so as to not get turned around for when I sleep at night that is when I am really watching when I am really not thinking at all when all there is to do is watch the star the one I am floating toward when I am awake there are simply too many distractions too many thoughts get in the way my thoughts get in the way just as they did in the case of my thoughts going off on a wild excursion and coming back with a translucent woolly mammoth this was some time after my strands of hair abandoned me once and for all my thoughts went off on excursion and came back with a translucent woolly mammoth a translucent woolly mammoth galloping toward me galloping toward me with the sole intention of befriending me a friendly translucent woolly mammoth which I thought at the time was not a friendly translucent woolly mammoth at all but simply my star the one in front simply a matter of my eyes becoming unfocused but which I soon realized had more than likely not been a matter of my eyes becoming unfocused but rather a matter of my thoughts getting in the way my thoughts had gotten in the way of the picture of my events the picture of my floating toward my star the word translucent and the word woolly and the word mammoth had suddenly popped into my head for no apparent reason had suddenly popped into my head because my thoughts had happened upon these words during an excursion my thoughts were off on an excursion in the wild and came across these words the word translucent and the word woolly and the word mammoth and these words got in the way of the picture of my events the friendly translucent woolly mammoth discovered by my thoughts while off on their wild excursion becoming part of my events or so it seemed to me which is very likely similar to that series of events leading up to my star the one in front of me my star having suddenly flickered off for a moment but instead of the words translucent woolly and mammoth my thoughts had discovered while on excursion the words flicker and off and these two words had become tangled up with my events in turn creating a distorted picture of my events the picture of which is supposed to be a picture of nothing but floating a picture of nothing at all but only of my stars the one in front the one behind it is impossible to know for sure to know what sorts of things what sorts of words my thoughts might encounter might stumble upon while on excursion but in any case my thoughts get in the way they get in the way except when I am dreaming except when I am sleeping at night when I sleep when I am dreaming I focus with all my strength on my star my thoughts cannot get in the way like they do in the day I try to think of a thought that has nothing to do with any word very difficult of course and of course I could have just as easily said night like they do in the night my thoughts cannot get in the way like they do in the night or like they do in the day by which I simply mean in either case that period during which I am not sleeping it is very difficult to clear my thoughts completely when I am not sleeping very difficult to concentrate on my star it is so much easier when I am dreaming when I am dreaming I am focusing only on my floating focusing only on my star the one in front focusing so to not get turned around yet I cannot clear my thoughts completely any longer no matter how hard I try not like before now I try to think to myself that my thoughts are completely empty I try to think there are no words no words at all yet there always seems to be a word popping up out of nowhere out of the emptiness the so called emptiness my thoughts are entirely empty I try to think entirely empty entirely empty my thoughts are entirely empty I try to think entirely empty my thoughts are entirely empty entirely empty my thoughts are entirely empty this is what I would think over and over again entirely empty entirely empty yet there have been words there all along all this while all this while I thought there was nothing all this while I thought my thoughts were entirely empty yet all this while there have been two words two words exactly empty of course the word empty and the word entirely those two words were there all along I thought there were no words yet there were in fact two of them this was not always the case shortly after I arrived here this was not quite as difficult after I arrived here it seemed I could go for a very long while without thinking I could clear my mind completely and think of nothing at all but now the only time when no words when no thoughts exist is during those periods of which I will later have no memory that is to say during those periods when I enter a state of unconsciousness or perhaps when I am asleep when I am dreaming when I am dreaming only of floating toward my star the one in front perhaps that is the only time when no words exist at all but of course I cannot be sure how do I know whether or not I am thinking of a word when I am sleeping when I am unconscious for example the word unconscious all that time I thought I was unconscious but I was thinking of the word unconscious over and over again the word unconscious the word unconscious unconscious unconscious unconscious of course I will have no memory of this no memory of what I was thinking all that time to either confirm or deny that I was thinking about the word unconscious but perhaps these are the moments these so called unconscious moments these moments of which I have no memory perhaps these are the moments when I am thinking most clearly thinking my most confident thoughts thinking very confidently thinking of absolutely nothing nothing to get in the way no words exist at all I cannot confirm or deny that these moments of which I will later have no memory are not in fact my most confident moments are not my greatest moments I can say with great confidence with the very greatest amount of confidence that these moments might be the moments of which I might be most proud the moments of which I might be able to say these moments might be my best moments these moments might be my very best moments of all for all these years these have been my best my most confident moments yet I have been able to go a long while quite a long while without thinking a single thought shortly after I arrived here shortly after my tears and strands of hair abandoned me once and for all there was a period during which I cleared my mind so completely so completely for a great number of years for many years it was only me and nothing the best of friends but of course something eventually snuck in some third party made its way in after so many years of clearing my mind completely after my long romance with nothing I have forgotten what exactly snuck in more than likely it concerned one of my stars either the one in front the one I am heading toward quarter of a fingernail or the one behind turning back now or perhaps it concerned something else perhaps some other third party snuck in perhaps what snuck in did not concern my star the one behind still a quarter of a fingernail or perhaps it did not now that I think of it I am quite certain that what snuck in turning back what snuck in did not concern my star after all these years I had forgotten what exactly snuck in but now I remember quarter of a fingernail as well I remember the one thing the one thing that snuck in was fleer the word fleer the third party was fleer the word fleer had snuck in fleer entered my mind very quickly leaving just as quickly then it was back to nothing my best friend nothing another epic romance during which I went many more years with no thoughts except for thoughts of nothing or to be accurate with no thoughts at all not even thoughts of nothing none whatsoever just me and nothing not one single thought not even fleer was able to get through during that subsequent period a great number of years yet I cannot remember why I chose to begin thinking again after such an extremely great number of years such an extremely great number of years after fleer perhaps I became bored or tired perhaps I became exhausted by the level of concentration necessary to maintain the absolute clearing of my mind I was more than likely simply exhausted after having concentrated for so many years on nothing rather not on nothing but not even on nothing so very exhausted by the effort required to maintain the great romance between us now I cannot go very long without thinking before it was easy but now I close my eyes try not to think and bang there is a thought a word bang the word pinecone pinecone another difficult subject pinecone is a very difficult a very painful subject because I cannot picture a pinecone I can only picture its word I do not know what the word means pinecone what the word pinecone points at for a great number of years there has been the word pinecone on the one hand and on the other hand also the word pinecone if I were to think of a word that does point at a thing other than its own word for example the word sneaker or the word fingernail if I were to think of speaking the word sneaker or the word fingernail as I often used to do many times in a row think of speaking the word fingernail exactly one thousand times in a row then during that period which would have been the one thousand and first time of thinking of speaking the word fingernail if during that period I only thought of the thing the word fingernail points at instead of thinking of speaking the word it would seem to me as if the word fingernail and the thing the word fingernail points at by which I mean the area below the tip of my finger it would seem to me that during this period of not thinking of speaking the word sneaker or the word fingernail but of only thinking of the thing the word sneaker or the word fingernail points at it would seem as if the word sneaker or the word fingernail pointed at the area near the tip of my finger in the case of the word fingernail or at one of my air jordans in the case of the word sneaker it would seem as if the word was pointing with less strength than it had one thousand fingernails or one thousand sneakers ago and when I thought of speaking the word fingernail or the word sneaker only five hundred times in a row instead of one thousand times in a row when I reached what would have been the five hundred and first time of thinking of speaking the word fingernail or the word sneaker I did not think of speaking it but only thought of what the word fingernail or the word sneaker points at that was when I noticed the word fingernail or the word sneaker was now pointing at the area near the tip of my finger in the case of the word fingernail or at one of my air jordans in the case of the word sneaker pointing with more or less twice as much strength as it had during the period which would have been the one thousand and first time of thinking of speaking the word fingernail or the word sneaker and this lessening the lessening of the strength of the word fingernail or the word sneaker to point at the thing it was supposed to point at by which I mean the area near the tip of my finger in the case of the word fingernail or one of my air jordans in the case of the word sneaker this lessening was something I felt I could count on something I could truly count on something I could truly depend on at the time this period of thinking of repeating the word fingernail or the word sneaker or the word pinecone having followed those acts of terrible abandonment committed against me by my tears and my strands of hair however when I conducted my repetitions upon the word pinecone when I thought of speaking the word pinecone many times in a row and I reached that point at which I had planned to only think of the thing the word pinecone is supposed to point at and not of thinking of speaking the word pinecone during the period which would have been the one thousand and first time or the ten thousand and first time or even the one hundred thousand and first time of thinking of speaking the word pinecone the word pinecone then pointed at the thing it was supposed to the thing corresponding to the firm area near the tip of my finger in the case of the word fingernail or one of my air jordans in the case of the word sneaker the word pinecone pointed at the thing it was supposed to point at with exactly the same amount of strength it had pointed at that thing after I had thought of speaking the word pinecone for the very first time which needless to say was with absolutely no strength at all there was no lessening of the strength with which the word pinecone pointed at the thing it was supposed to point at even during the period which would have been the one hundred thousand and first time of thinking of speaking the word pinecone because the word pinecone had never pointed at the thing it was supposed to point at with any strength at all unlike the word fingernail or the word sneaker which at first pointed at the area near the tip of my finger in the case of the word fingernail or at one of my air jordans in the case of the word sneaker pointed very strongly only later to lose its strength to do so and so I felt that I had one very dependable friend in the ability of the strength of the word fingernail or the word sneaker to lessen and another very dependable friend in the inability of the strength of the word pinecone to lessen two very dependable friends for a great number of years this is how it was for me with the word pinecone the word pinecone on the one hand and on the other hand the word pinecone or the word pinecone on the one hand and on the other hand nothing at all for a great number of years this is how it was until one day or one night I often imagine this happened at night until one night or one day when I had reached my sixty eight thousand nine hundred and sixty eighth repetition of thinking of speaking the word pinecone what happened was that after I had thought of speaking the word pinecone for the sixty eight thousand nine hundred and sixty eighth time at precisely that number of pinecones I felt an urgent need to stop short of my goal of one hundred thousand and immediately stop thinking of speaking the word pinecone after the sixty eight thousand nine hundred and sixty eighth pinecone it suddenly occurred to me that I should simply attempt to think of the thing the word is supposed to point at without thinking of speaking the word exactly what I had planned to do during that period in which I would have thought of speaking the word pinecone for the one hundred thousand and first time but it was during this period of thinking of the thing the word pinecone is supposed to point at without thinking of speaking the word pinecone during the period in which I would have thought of speaking the word pinecone for the sixty eight thousand nine hundred and sixty ninth time that the word pinecone seemed to me to suddenly point with less strength at the thing it was supposed to point at the thing corresponding to the area near the tip of my finger in the case of the word fingernail that is to say the real pinecone the actual thing I had entirely forgotten it was during this period that it suddenly became clear to me that the word pinecone had begun pointing to the nothing it was supposed to point at with even less strength than it had previously pointed to that same nothing which is not to say that the word pinecone had begun pointing with more strength at the thing I had forgotten at the actual pinecone no that is not what happened at all what happened was that the word pinecone had suddenly begun to point at what I previously thought was nothing with even less strength than it had pointed at nothing before it was as if the word pinecone itself had lost some of its strength to even be meaningless and now I was perhaps beginning to lose some of the meaninglessness of the word itself I was somehow beginning to lose that very dependable friend represented by the inability of the strength of the word pinecone to lessen as if the word pinecone had begun to lose even its strength to be an entirely meaningless word which is not to say that the word had become more meaningful no not at all but only that the word pinecone had become less meaningless without becoming more meaningful and also without become more meaningless as if not only had I lost the thing the word pinecone was supposed to point at not only had I lost a dependable friend in the inability of the strength of the word to lessen but I was perhaps well on my way to losing the word itself as if were I to continue with my repetitions were I to proceed to conduct my repetitions upon the word pinecone even a single repetition more I might very well lose the word pinecone entirely it was as if I had taken that nothing which the word pinecone had previously pointed at and I had chopped off a certain percentage of it perhaps even half the old nothing was now gone perhaps more it was as if I had chopped the legs off my best friend my best friend nothing as if I had created a new nothing somehow less than the old nothing I had begun with as if what I had previously thought of as nothing as simply my old friend nothing now seemed to me to be very much something as if I had been deceiving myself all these years when conducting my repetitions upon the word pinecone for I had never turned to look at that so called nothing square in the face as if I was finally able to see that nothing being nothing and that being the end of it was incorrect and now after having failed to see this little something in the nothing having failed to turn and look at my old friend nothing square in the face

I saw that the something I had not seen in that old nothing was already almost gone and my old friend nothing which was actually something all this while all these many years for an extremely great number of years that old nothing was quickly becoming absolutely nothing at all it was as if the word nothing that same word I had always used to describe the thing representing the total lack of everything with regard to my knowledge of what the word pinecone was supposed to point at that same nothing I considered my very best friend for so many years as if this old word as if this old nothing as if this old friend would no longer have the strength to describe the new and greater and purer nothing this absolute stranger I now saw right in front of me as if my old nothing had all at once stopped pointing at that thing corresponding to the area near the tip of my finger in the case of the word fingernail but now pointed at something even less than nothing now pointed at hardly any nothing at all suffice to say I permanently discontinued my repetitions feeling that I was fortunate to be able to still say although there is now a nothing even less of something than nothing there is still a little nothing left I felt very fortunate to be able to still say there is still enough nothing to recognize the new nothing as a kind of nothing as at least a version of my old friend nothing my faithful companion extremely fortunate to be able to say of this new nothing while it is a much deeper or much slighter kind of nothing perhaps a much truer or a much falser kind of nothing it is still a kind of nothing nonetheless and that is still something fortunate because I still have a friend perhaps not a true friend but a friend nonetheless in this slighter or truer or falser or purer kind of nothing still a friend not quite my old friend nothing but perhaps a new friend my new friend not even nothing my new friend less than nothing but of course just as it is with my arms with my legs with my sneakers and so forth I cannot consider nothing I cannot consider nothing or less than nothing my friend in the true sense the true meaning of the word friend the word friendship what I would give for a true friend a real friend a reciprocal friendship I cannot remember ever having been party to a true friendship a friendship according to the true meaning of the word I cannot remember having been party to such a friendship on the roof where I was before I cannot remember ever saying of so and so yes this is my friend I cannot remember ever saying or thinking or thinking of saying I count this particular so and so among my friends among my very dearest friends I cannot remember ever asking someone would you like to go see a what is it called or would you like to go to a baseball card convention with me I cannot remember ever doing anything of the sort however I can remember coming into contact with people coming into contact with various people or perhaps one person perhaps a single person near my parents what is it called coming into contact with a person perhaps a neighbor coming into contact with a person who was likely a neighbor I saw the likely neighbor from my perspective on the roof I cannot see this neighbor now I cannot see the likely neighbor I cannot see the face or the body the arms or the legs or the fingernails or even the sneakers however I am relatively confident of having come into contact with a neighbor of some sort I believe I may have even spoken to this neighbor to the likely neighbor I believe I spoke to the likely neighbor at least once while atop my parents roof I do not recall the name of the likely neighbor I remember nothing whatsoever of the appearance of the face of the hands the sneakers or the fingernails of the likely neighbor but I am relatively confident that this person the one person I came into contact with was more than likely a neighbor at the very least a person who happened at one point to walk past my parents what is it called a person who would have been visible to me from my position atop the roof this I remember quite clearly I quite clearly remember the likely neighbor walking past my parents what is it called toward some destination in the distance perhaps toward the far end of the path I remember the likely neighbor turning toward me toward my position atop the roof the likely neighbor being not so far away that the voice of the likely neighbor could not be heard by me by my ears from their position atop the roof for I do remember the voice of the likely neighbor as the likely neighbor turned to face me turned toward me toward my position on the roof to say nice day I remember the voice of the likely neighbor saying nice day and then my own voice my own voice replying I am sure of it I am quite certain my voice said something in reply yet I do not remember exactly what words my voice used in reply to the voice of the likely neighbor I have often imagined that I agreed with the likely neighbor I have often imagined I agreed with the likely neighbor that yes it was in fact a nice day I have imagined this for it would be in keeping with my character it would be in keeping with my nature to offer such a reply even if in fact it was not a nice day even if it was raining and the likely neighbor walking along the path before my parents what is it called had turned toward me turned toward my position on the roof to say nice day even in spite of it not being a nice day even in spite of the likely neighbor being drenched by the rain I have often imagined that I would have more than likely agreed with the likely neighbor I have imagined many times that I would have more than likely agreed that yes it was in fact a nice day my agreement with the likely neighbor being in that case more a matter of courtesy a matter of preserving the possibility of a friendship with the likely neighbor more a matter of courtesy than a matter of preserving the possibility of being truthful about the condition about the quality of the day I have often imagined myself more than likely having agreed with the likely neighbor that yes it was a nice day more than likely having said yes or having said yes I agree with you likely neighbor or having said yes you are correct in so saying it is indeed a truly nice day having very often imagined myself having likely said yes you are correct likely neighbor in fact I would even go so far as to call it a splendid day or more than likely replied to the likely neighbor that it is a marvelous day more than likely yes likely neighbor although it is raining today it is indeed a very nice day yes likely neighbor yes although it is raining buckets you are perfectly correct in calling this a nice day for all days are nice in some way or yes likely neighbor terrifically nice I have even imagined my voice replying to the voice of the likely neighbor that this is in fact the nicest day in the history of the world I have often imagined I would have said this or something to this effect I would have agreed with the likely neighbor in spite of rain or hail on that day for in so doing for in so saying I would preserve the possibility of our friendship as opposed to the mere possibility of being truthful about the quality of the day however I would have been outright lying in saying it was a nice day or an extremely nice day or the very nicest day in the history of the world in the event of a hailstorm such a reply would represent an outright lie in the event of a hailstorm I would have been lying had I exclaimed the niceness of the day to the likely neighbor as hail fell between us I would have agreed with the likely neighbor in that case only in hope of beginning a friendship between us only because I would be willing to lie to the likely neighbor in order to make the likely neighbor feel that I am someone whose opinion about the quality of the day accords with the opinion held by the likely neighbor because if we were to share an opinion about the quality of the day perhaps we might share other opinions many other opinions and perhaps the likely neighbor and I will go on to become great friends on account of the many opinions we share the great number of opinions on various topics ranging from the quality of the day to many other things besides the weather perhaps even baseball cards I have often imagined the likely neighbor and I engaging in a true friendship in which we regularly meet to discuss baseball cards or even to trade baseball cards the likely neighbor and I trading baseball cards the likely neighbor and I sitting on the staircase and trading our baseball cards lining them up in rows to decide which ones we want which ones we need which ones we can spare which ones we have always wanted trading baseball cards on the stairs carpeted stairs a carpeted staircase placing no more than twelve baseball cards on each step on each carpeted step six cards on the left side of each step six cards on the right in order to leave a pathway through the middle of the staircase just large enough for us to continue walking up and down the stairs taking our time to examine the cards to choose our favorites we will trade baseball cards on the stairs turning back the likely neighbor and I turning back to measure and then later we might even go outside go for a walk perhaps holding hands quarter of a fingernail walking along the path in front of my parents what is it called holding hands in the hail turning back walking toward a baseball card convention in the middle distance great friends quarter of a fingernail as well the very greatest of friends holding hands and avoiding the hail what I would give what I would give now to hold a hand the hand of the likely neighbor to hold a hand in my hand to hold a different hand than my own hand in my hand to hold a hand in both of my hands perhaps to take a hand and to hold that hand between my own two hands and to hold that different hand before me before my eyes before my eyes against the light from my star the one in front in order to carefully examine that different hand keeping an eye out for distinguishing features to distinguish among the features of the different hand and the features of my own hand to keep a list of the features distinguishing our hands a list of the differences that make our hands unique to keep a list on a piece of paper and to add to the list over the years as our hands age as our hands become different or perhaps even become similar to keep two lists two lists on two different pieces of paper one list listing the differences between our hands the other list listing the similarities between our hands two lists on two different pieces of paper as well as a third list a third list listing the differences between our feet three lists on three different pieces of paper as well as a fourth list on a fourth piece of paper a fourth list listing the differences between our hands one list on one piece of paper listing the similarities between our hands one list on another piece of paper listing the differences between our feet and one list on yet another piece of paper listing the similarities between our feet making five lists total five different pieces of paper and then also another list on another piece of paper listing the similarities between our noses six lists including a list listing the differences between our noses as well as those five lists mentioned previously eight lists then all on different pieces of paper including those lists mentioned previously as well as two more lists listing the similarities between our eyes which would make thirteen lists including those lists mentioned previously as well as another two two more lists on two more separate pieces of paper listing the differences between our eyes and our ears and a list listing all of the similarities between our hair as well as lists listing the similarities between our ears our teeth and our lips as well as a list listing the differences between our hair making fifty lists total on fifty different pieces of paper not yet including the following additional lists listing the differences between our teeth our lips our necks our heads our elbows and our shoulders bringing the total number of lists up to ninety ninety lists on ninety pieces of paper without having yet included those lists listing the similarities between our necks our heads our elbows our shoulders our fingers our toes our eyelashes our navels our nipples our buttocks our eyebrows our fingernails our forearms our knees and our knuckles as well as the differences between our fingers our eyelashes our navels our buttocks our nipples our toes our fingernails our eyebrows our forearms our knees our knuckles and our toenails as well as of course a list listing the similarities between our toenails which brings the total number of necessary lists up to three hundred and twenty four on three hundred and twenty four separate pieces of paper which the likely neighbor and I might share and often refer to throughout the course of our friendship yet I have often imagined I have often imagined and I have often dreaded the possibility that the likely neighbor would not be willing to engage in a friendship with me in the first place I have dreaded the possibility of the likely neighbor not responding as positively as I had hoped upon my agreement with the likely neighbor as to the quality of the day if for example the likely neighbor had said nice day as it was hailing and I agreed that yes in fact it is a very nice day the very nicest day in the history of the world when in fact the likely neighbor meant to suggest the exact opposite the likely neighbor meant to suggest as hail fell between us as hail fell upon the head of the likely neighbor perhaps even injuring the head of the likely neighbor as the likely neighbor remarked that today is a nice day the likely neighbor in fact meant to suggest that today is the very worst day not a nice day at all in fact today is the very worst day in the history of the world and yet I had responded under the impression that the likely neighbor did in fact believe it to be a very nice day and in so responding I could have been mistaken to suggest that I did not care whether hail was falling upon and injuring the head of the likely neighbor that I in fact approved of these injuries by shouting out at the likely neighbor from my position atop the roof yes what a nice day yes likely neighbor I am glad that hail is falling upon your head and injuring it and also injuring your body in which case the likely neighbor would feel compelled to continue walking along the path past my parents what is it called without giving me a second thought without giving the possibility of our friendship what could have been a great friendship in which we often traded baseball cards on the stairs without giving the possibility of what could have been the greatest friendship in the history of the world even the slightest consideration but instead imagining me as someone who appreciates or even enjoys the sight of the likely neighbor being terribly injured someone who enjoys the sight of the head and the body of the likely neighbor being injured by hail it is the kind of thought the thought of the likely neighbor disapproving of my response never giving the possibility of our friendship a second thought but instead walking along the path toward the baseball card convention alone it is the kind of thought which if my ducts had not gone dry would even today even tonight the thought would make me cry before my ducts went dry shortly after I arrived here even before the period during which I concentrated my efforts exclusively upon the nature of empty space even before the period during which I conversed with my tears there was a period during which I simply cried that is all I cried I cried at first because I was scared because I was scared and lonely and only much later did I cry because I found that my tears floated alongside me to become my very greatest friends so in the latter case I cried not in sadness but in joy and in this joy in this latter kind of crying I created more friends and even later I cried neither from sadness nor from joy but only from the desire to produce more tears to produce more friends I cried only to cry myself more friends and soon thereafter my ducts went dry I lost my ability to cry it was a dryness which of course saddened me considerably but also awakened in me the understanding that those tears I did cry were great gifts the very greatest and rarest gifts having floated alongside me for such a great length of time they were indeed my faithful companions my good friends but then they suddenly disappeared they abandoned me and I would have cried how I would have cried over this act of absolute abandonment had my ducts not gone dry I would have cried an ocean of tears and even now even today or tonight I would cry an ocean if I could but of course my ducts are dry I can only cry on the inside I can always cry on the inside shortly after I arrived here before I cried to produce more friends before I cried in joy I cried because I was scared because I was scared and lonely and also because I had become convinced that I was stuck in the middle stuck between my stars I was convinced that I was not moving that I was caught right in the middle where the gravities from the two stars met in a tug of war I wept and wept and my tears floated alongside me I pedaled my feet and I flapped my arms I wept and wept I continued crying until one day or one night my thoughts went on an excursion it was a preliminary excursion they went off on an excursion just as they would later go off on an excursion in the wild to discover the word translucent and the word woolly and the word mammoth in the case of the friendly translucent woolly mammoth galloping toward me and even later to discover the word flicker and the word off in the case of my star the one in front having momentarily flickered off but while on excursion this time on this preliminary excursion they stumbled upon a word a single word the word friend the picture of my events the picture of my floating became momentarily tangled up with my thoughts for a moment only for a moment instead of my tears floating by my side instead I saw something else just as I would later see a translucent woolly mammoth galloping toward me and even later my star flickering off in this case however instead of my tears floating by my side instead of my thousands upon thousands of tears I perceived something else my tears momentarily ceased to be tears to be merely tears I momentarily perceived them to be friends my friends the truest of friends I momentarily perceived thousands upon thousands upon millions upon billions of people friends all true friends all floating alongside all of us together they were true reciprocal friendships if only for a moment a very brief moment my tears had become real people real friends true friends in the true meaning of the word friend the word friendship and we all floated together if only for the briefest of moments perhaps only for a single second I floated alongside my millions upon billions of great old friends dear friends all of us holding hands and although my tears immediately thereafter went back to just being tears and would later abandon me it was perhaps this momentary vision of floating alongside so many true friends that made everything thereafter including my tears and my strands of hair abandoning me as well as my loss of the questioning nature of my positively hopeless questions as well as the word pinecone losing its strength to point at nothing my old friend nothing as well as the continued possibility of the likely neighbor not wanting to trade baseball cards on the stairs this single moment of my mistaken perception a moment of my mistakenly perceiving my tears as real people as true friends perhaps this is what allowed everything else to be tolerable not tolerable perhaps not quite tolerable because in fact so much of it was intolerable absolutely intolerable so much of it remains absolutely intolerable yet I was still able to endure turning back I was and still am able to endure perhaps endure is the correct word no matter what happened or what happens or what will happen or what will not happen quarter of a fingernail it was this single moment perhaps a mere second of perceiving myself of mistakenly perceiving myself not among an ocean of tears but among an ocean of true friends that has made it possible turning back and will continue to make it possible for me to endure to keep floating toward my star the one in front quarter of a fingernail as well

ABOUT THE AUTHOR

Evan Lavender-Smith attended the University of California, Berkeley. He is the author of *From Old Notebooks* (BlazeVOX, 2010).

9032077R0

Made in the USA
Charleston, SC
05 August 2011